THE RETURN
of
THE HERO

Illustrated by ERIC KINCAID
Story adapted by JUNE WOODMAN

BRIMAX BOOKS   NEWMARKET   ENGLAND

Toad was a very good fellow, but he just could not help being boastful. His friend the Water Rat tried to make him see that there was nothing to be proud of in stealing cars, being in prison, and upsetting all his friends.

"I suppose you're right; I've been a bit of a fool," sighed Toad, while secretly thinking what fun it had all been. "But now I'm back from my adventures, I'll settle down and be a dull sort of fellow if that's what you really want. Let's stroll gently down to Toad Hall, shall we?"

"What are you talking about?" cried the Rat, excitedly. "Haven't you heard?"

"Heard what?" said Toad, turning pale.

"The stoats and weasels have taken Toad Hall!" shouted Rat.

Toad leaned his chin on his paws; two tears splashed onto the table, plop! plop! "Tell me all, I can bear it," he sobbed.

"When you were in prison the Wild Wood animals said you'd *never* come back. But your good friends Mole and Badger said you *would*, sometime, somehow. So they stayed on to look after your home. But one night, hundreds of stoats and weasels attacked the Hall and threw them out!"

Ratty told him that the Wild Wooders had been living there ever since. "Lying in bed half the day," he went on, "and the place in such a mess. Eating your food, drinking your drink, and singing rude songs about thieves and prisons. They say they're staying for good!"

"O, do they?" cried Toad, seizing a stick. "We'll see about that!"

"It's no good, Toad," called Ratty. But Toad was off.

When Toad got to his own front gate an armed ferret was on guard. Without a word, he raised his gun and fired. BANG!

Toad ran for his life. Mocking laughter followed him.

10

He went glumly back and told Ratty. "What did I tell you?" cried the Rat. "They're armed to the teeth!"

Still, Toad wasn't going to give in. He got out Rat's boat and rowed to the Hall. Everything seemed quiet. He drifted on cautiously and was just under the bridge when . . . CRASH! . . . a great stone was dropped from above – it smashed through the bottom of the boat and sank it.

Struggling in the water, Toad looked up to see two stoats leaning over the bridge watching him. "It'll be your head next time!" they taunted, giggling.

Sadly, Toad went back to tell Ratty.

"*What* did I tell you?" said Ratty crossly. "It's a wonder you've got any friends left." Toad apologised humbly about the boat and promised to do nothing else without Rat's kind advice and approval.

They were just sitting down to eat when who should arrive but Badger, closely followed by Mole. They looked very dirty and untidy. They had been sleeping rough while keeping an eye on Toad Hall. Toad started to giggle.

"You don't deserve such loyal friends," whispered Ratty sharply.

But dear Moly was delighted to see Toad. "Hooray! Here's clever Toad back again!" he cried, dancing round. Toad began to swell with pride.

While Mole and Badger ate supper, Toad began boasting of his adventures.

"Toad, do be quiet," said Ratty. "And don't you egg him on, Mole. Now let's decide what's to be done now Toad is back at last. I think he should . . ."

"No he shouldn't!" cried Mole. "He should . . ."

"Well, I shan't!" shouted Toad. "I won't be bossed about by you! I shall . . ."

By now, all three were shouting together. Suddenly a stern voice said, "Be quiet at once!" It was Badger. Not another word was said until he had finished eating. Then Badger stood up and told them what was to be done.

"Toad," said the Badger, "you're a bad, troublesome little animal!" Toad started to sob.

"Don't cry," said Badger more kindly. "I'll tell you a great secret. There – is – an – underground – passage. It runs from here into the middle of Toad Hall!"

"O, nonsense Badger," sobbed Toad.

"Your father told me," said Badger, "but he said not to tell you unless you were in a real fix because you can't keep secrets." Toad went a bit sulky.

Badger then said Otter had disguised himself as a sweep and called at Toad Hall. "He discovered that tomorrow's a big feast," said Badger. "It's the Chief Weasel's birthday."

"They'll all be in the Hall, eating and drinking, no guns or weapons at all," went on the Badger.

"But the guards will be armed," said Ratty.

"Exactly," smiled Badger, "but we shall go in *underneath* the armed guards!"

"Then rush out on those weasels!" cried Mole.

"And whack'em and whack'em!" shouted Toad, running round the room and jumping over the chairs in great excitement.

"That's settled then," said Badger. "Everyone off to bed."

It was late when Toad got down next day to find Badger reading quietly, Ratty piling up weapons and Mole off by himself somewhere.

Presently, Mole came tumbling in. "I've been to Toad Hall, dressed up in the washerwoman's clothes!" he cried.

"I hope you were careful, Mole?" said the Rat.

"I hope so too," laughed Mole. "I said, 'Want any washing done?' 'Run away,' said the stoat guards. 'You'll be running soon,' I said. And I told them a hundred bloodthirsty badgers, six boatloads of rats with pistols, and a great army of Death-or-Glory toads would attack them tonight! They all ran around in a panic, giving each other orders. Then they said it was just like those weasels to have a party and leave them to be cut to pieces."

"You *fool*!" cried Toad. "You've spoilt everything!"

But Badger spoke up firmly. "Mole, you have more sense in your little finger than some animals have in the whole of their fat bodies. Clever Mole!"

The Toad was wild with jealousy. Fortunately for him, before he could give way to his temper, it was time for lunch. Afterwards, Mr. Badger settled down for forty winks. Ratty got on with sorting out piles of weapons, saying, "A-pistol-for-Toad, a-pistol-for-Mole, a-pistol-for-Badger . . ." and so on.

So Mole took Toad outside, sat him down, and kindly let him tell all his adventures over again, from beginning to end.

When it began to grow dark, an excited Rat called them all inside. He stood each one beside a little heap of weapons and proceeded to dress them up. Each had a belt, with sword and pistol, handcuffs, sticking plaster and a big stick.

Mr. Badger laughed and said all he needed was a big stick. But Ratty said he didn't want to get the blame afterwards for forgetting anything.

When all was ready, Badger took up his lantern, grasped his great stick and said, "Follow me! Mole first, Rat next and Toad last. And don't chatter, Toady, or you'll be sent back!"

Silently the animals set off in line; Badger led them along the river bank until he came to a hole. He swung himself into it, closely followed by Mole and Ratty. Then Toad managed to slip into the water with a loud splash. He was hauled out, rubbed down and comforted.

Then, at last, they were all in the secret tunnel and the adventure had really begun. As they crept quietly along the narrow tunnel, Toad bumped into the others. Badger thought they were under attack and nearly put a bullet into Toad.

"That tiresome Toad shall be left behind!" cried Badger.

But the others promised to watch him and they all moved on.

Suddenly, overhead, they heard a noise – as if people were shouting, cheering and celebrating. They heard a clinking of glasses.

"What a time they're having!" said the Badger. They hurried on until they got to the trap-door. "Now, boys, all together, heave!" said the Badger as they lifted the trap-door. They climbed through into the pantry but no one heard them. The weasels were making too much noise, singing rude songs about Toad.

Then Badger cried, "The hour is come! Follow me!" He flung the door open wide.

My!

What a squealing and a screeching filled the air! Terrified weasels dived under tables, tried to climb the walls and got stuck in the chimney! Tables and chairs were upset, glasses and china crashed to the floor. There was complete panic when those four heroes strode into the Hall.

There was mighty Badger, his great stick whistling through the air; Mole, black and grim, shouting his war-cry, "A Mole! A Mole!" Rat, desperate and determined, his belt bulging with weapons, attacking fiercely; and Toad, frenzied with excitement, swollen to twice his normal size, crying Toad-whoops that chilled the weasels to the marrow as he struck out.

There were only four of them, but to the panic-stricken weasels they seemed to be everywhere. The weasels fled this way and that – anywhere to escape those dreadful sticks.

The affair was soon over. Up and down the hall strode the four friends, whacking their sticks at every head that showed itself.

In five minutes the room was cleared. Badger asked the Mole to go and see what the stoats on sentry-duty were doing.

"Not that I think we'll have much trouble from them tonight, thanks to you," he added. Then he got the others to pick up a table and some chairs.

"Stir your stumps, Toad," grumbled Badger. "We've got your house back for you, now we want some grub!"

Toad felt rather hurt. He'd been specially pleased with himself when he had gone for the Chief Weasel and sent him flying, but Badger never praised him as he did the Mole. Still, he and Ratty bustled about, collecting chicken, trifle, rolls and cheese.

Just then, Mole clambered back through the window, with an armful of rifles. "It's all over," he reported. "Most of them threw down their rifles and fled. The ones who stayed, got into fights when the weasels came rushing out. Lots of 'em ended up in the river!"

"Excellent animal!" said the Badger. "Just one more thing – get those captured stoats to sweep out the bedrooms and make up all our beds with clean sheets, will you?"

So the good-natured Mole picked up his stick, formed the prisoners into a line and said, "Quick march!"

Soon he was back, reporting that every room was ready, and that he had let the prisoners go. As he pulled up a chair to eat, Toad, forgetting his jealousy thanked him very much for everything, and especially for his great cleverness that morning. Badger was pleased at that, saying, "Well spoken, my brave Toad!"

Next morning, it was decided to have a celebration banquet. Badger told Toad to write out all the invitations.

"What! Stop indoors on a fine day like this?" moaned Toad. Then a sudden thought struck him, and he changed his tune. "Of course, Badger – anything to give my friends pleasure!" he smiled.

Badger looked very suspicious, but Toad hurried off and settled down at his writing table. Here was his chance to tell all the river folk about his adventures and the fine, brave things he had done. First he listed the programme of entertainment:
a speech – by Toad; then a song – by Toad; then a poem . . .

A rather scruffy weasel was only too eager to deliver the invitations. But Badger and Ratty soon discovered the weasel and took the disgraceful cards away from him. Mole went off to write some more.

Badger and Ratty cornered poor Toad and reminded him sternly that he had promised to change his ways. He was very downhearted about it but finally he agreed to keep his promise and went sadly to his room. Once there, he dressed and then arranged all the chairs in front of him. To an empty room, Toad sang one last conceited song. Then he sighed and went down to the banquet.

The banquet was a great success and all Toad's friends gathered round, praising his cleverness. But Toad stayed quiet and humble. Badger and Ratty were so surprised at his good behaviour they sat with their mouths open – which pleased Toad greatly. Even when somebody called, "Speech! Speech!" he just shook his head modestly.

He was indeed an altered Toad!

Toad's last tasks were to reward the gaoler's daughter and the engine-driver. Badger also made him pay the bargewoman for her horse.

Sometimes the four friends would stroll in the Wild Wood, now tamed, or go boating on the river. Wherever they went, they were never far from the pleasant sound of the wind in the willows.

Stories from
The Wind in the Willows
by
KENNETH GRAHAME

ISBN 0 86112 450 2

© Brimax Books Ltd 1987
All rights reserved
Published by Brimax Books, Newmarket, England 1987
Printed in Hong Kong